A Beginning-to-Read Book

Dear Dragon Goes to the Firehouse

by Margaret Hillert
Illustrated by David Schimmell

NORWOOD HOUSE PRESS

DEAR CAREGIVER,

The *Beginning-to-Read* series is a carefully written collection of classic readers you may remember from your own childhood. Each book features text comprised of common sight words to provide your child ample practice reading the words that appear most frequently in written text. The many additional details in the pictures enhance the story and offer the opportunity for you to help your child expand oral language and develop comprehension.

Begin by reading the story to your child, followed by letting him or her read familiar words and soon your child will be able to read the story independently. At each step of the way, be sure to praise your reader's efforts to build his or her confidence as an independent reader. Discuss the pictures and encourage your child to make connections between the story and his or her own life. At the end of the story, you will find reading activities and a word list that will help your child practice and strengthen beginning reading skills.

Above all, the most important part of the reading experience is to have fun and enjoy it!

Shannon Cannon

Shannon Cannon,
Literacy Consultant

Norwood House Press • P.O. Box 316598 • Chicago, Illinois 60631
For more information about Norwood House Press please visit our website at *www.norwoodhousepress.com* or call 866-565-2900.

Special thanks to Gayle Vaul-Kennedy of the Chicago Fire Department.

LIBRARY OF CONGRESS CATALOGING-IN-PUBLICATION DATA
Hillert, Margaret.
  Dear dragon goes to the firehouse / by Margaret Hillert ; illustrated by David Schimmell.
    p. cm. -- (A beginning-to-read book)
  Summary: "A boy and his pet dragon go on a class trip to the local fire house and learn about what it takes to put out a fire"--Provided by publisher.
    ISBN-13: 978-1-59953-375-9 (library edition : alk. paper)
    ISBN-10: 1-59953-375-8 (library edition : alk. paper)
  [1. Fire departments--Fiction. 2. Dragons--Fiction.] I. Schimmell, David, ill. II. Title.
  PZ7.H558Def 2010
  [E]--dc22
                              2009042919

Manufactured in the United States of America in North Mankato, Minnesota. 160N—072010

It is a good day for a walk.
We will go for a walk and—
Guess what?

We will see something big.
A big thing that is a good help to us.

Here we go.
We will walk and walk and walk.
A walk is good for us.

Look up there.
It is red so we have to STOP.

Now it is GREEN.
So we can GO, GO, GO.
Come on.
Come on.

7

Here we are.
This is the firehouse.

O-o-o-h—
Look at that.
So big. So BIG.

No.1

E-1

Yes, it is.
And it is a big help to us.

Come in.
Come in.
We are happy to see you.

When we go to a fire we
put on this—
    and this—
        and this.

And to help us put out a fire,
we have to have this—
and this—
and this.

Oh, look at the dog.
Is it a fire dog?
Is it?

No. He is a friend.
He does not work.
He likes it here.
We give him things to eat.

Put this on.
See how you look.

Oh, no.
This is not good.
It is too big for me.

I have something for you.
One for you—
        and you—
            and you.

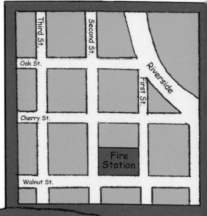

Ooooooh!
Fire hats.
Red fire hats.

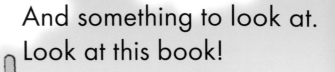

And something to look at.
Look at this book!

Do not play with fire.

This is so big and red.
Can we go up there?

Yes. Yes.
Go up.
Up, Up, Up!

Now we have to go.
It was fun to be here.
But now we have to go.

Here I am with you.
And here you are with me.
What fun.
What fun, dear dragon.

The following activities support the findings of the National Reading Panel that determined the most effective components for reading instruction are: Phonemic Awareness, Phonics, Vocabulary, Fluency, and Text Comprehension.

Phonemic Awareness: The /o/ sound

Sound Substitution: Say the following words to your child and ask him or her to substitute the middle sound in the word with **/o/**:

tip = top	seed = sod	luck = lock	jig = jog
sick = sock	leg = log	step = stop	ship = shop
pat = pot	dill = doll	let = lot	rib = rob
fix = fox	tick = tock	deck = dock	

Phonics: The letters O and o

1. Demonstrate how to form the letters **O** and **o** for your child.

2. Have your child practice writing **O** and **o** at least three times each.

3. Write down the following letters and spaces and ask your child to write the letter **o** on the spaces in each word:

bl_ck	st_p	m_m	m_p	j_b
d_t	t_p	sh_p	cl_ck	dr_p
fr_g	tr_t	h_t	l_g	kn_ck
n_t	s_ck	g_t		

Vocabulary: Concept Words

1. Write the following words on separate pieces of paper and point to them as you read them to your child:

truck	hose	firefighter
boots	helmet	flames

2. Say the following sentences aloud and ask your child to point to the word that is described:

- This is a person who puts out fires. (firefighter)
- Firefighters wear these to keep their feet and legs safe. (boots)
- This is what firefighters wear to protect their heads. (helmet)
- Firefighters ride on this to get to the fire. (truck)
- The fire truck has a very big one of these to get water to the fire. (hose)
- The hose helps firefighters put these out. (flames)

Fluency: Shared Reading/CLOZE

1. Reread the story with your child at least two more times while your child tracks the print by running a finger under the words as they are read. Ask your child to read the words he or she knows with you.

2. Reread the story, stopping occasionally so your child can supply the next word. For example, *We will see something _____* (big), or *It is red so we have to _____* (stop), or *Do not play with _____* (fire).

3. Now have your child reread the story, stopping occasionally for you to supply the next word.

Text Comprehension: Discussion Time

1. Ask your child to retell the sequence of events in the story.

2. To check comprehension, ask your child the following questions:

- What color on the light means it is safe to walk?
- What do firefighters wear? Why?
- Why did Dear Dragon laugh at the boy?
- What did the firefighter give the kids?

WORD LIST

***Dear Dragon Goes to the Firehouse* uses the 76 pre-primer vocabulary words listed below**. This list can be used to practice reading the words that appear in the text. You may wish to write the words on index cards and use them to help your child build automatic word recognition. Regular practice with these words will enhance your child's fluency in reading connected text.

a	dragon	he	oh	this
am		help	on	to
and	eat	here	one	too
are		him	out	
at	fire	how		up
	firehouse		play	us
be	for	I	put	
big	friend	in		walk
book	fun	is	red	was
but		it		we
	give	like(s)	see	what
can	go	look	so	when
come	good		something	will
	green	me	stop	with
day	guess			work
dear		no	that	
do	happy	not	the	yes
does	hats	now	there	you
dog	have		thing(s)	

ABOUT THE AUTHOR   Margaret Hillert has written over 80 books for children who are just learning to read. Her books have been translated into many different languages and over a million children throughout the world have read her books. She first started writing poetry as a child and has continued to write for children and adults throughout her life. A first grade teacher for 34 years, Margaret is now retired from teaching and lives in Michigan where she likes to write, take walks in the morning, and care for her three cats.

Photograph by Glenna Washburn

ABOUT THE ADVISER   Shannon Cannon contributed the activities pages that appear in this book. Shannon serves as a literacy consultant and provides staff development to help improve reading instruction. She is a frequent presenter at educational conferences and workshops. Prior to this she worked as an elementary school teacher and as president of a curriculum publishing company.